EMPIRES IN LOVE AND WAR

TUSHAR RAJ

Made with ♥ on the Notion Press Platform
www.notionpress.com

To my grandparents, who taught me the love of history and storytelling. Your tales of the past inspired me to imagine the lives of those who came before us and to bring their stories to life. Your unwavering support and encouragement have been a constant source of strength and inspiration throughout my journey as a writer.

To all the brave men and women who lived during the rise and fall of empires, who fought for their beliefs, and who loved amidst the chaos of war. This book is dedicated to you, and to your legacy of strength, courage, and enduring love.

And finally, to my readers. Thank you for taking the time to join me on this journey through history. I hope this story will spark your imagination, inspire you, and provide a glimpse into the lives of those who lived in a world much different than our own.

With gratitude and admiration,

Tushar Raj

Contents

Foreword

Dear Readers,

Welcome to "Empires in Love and War," a historical fiction novel that explores the rise and fall of empires through the lens of love and war. This book is a result of my passion for history and my love for storytelling. I hope to bring you on a journey that transports you to another time and place, where you can experience the challenges and triumphs of our ancestors.

The pages of this book are filled with drama, romance, and adventure, as we follow the lives of characters who are caught in the middle of the great events that shaped the world. From the rise of powerful empires to their ultimate downfall, this story covers it all. Throughout the book, you'll encounter memorable characters, including warriors, statesmen, and everyday people who lived through the times.

This novel also explores the interplay between love and war, two of the most powerful and enduring human experiences. You'll see how love can bring people together, even in the midst of the greatest conflict, and how war can tear apart even the strongest of relationships. By examining these themes, we can better understand the complexities of human nature and the world we live in.

I believe that history is not just a collection of dry facts and dates, but a rich tapestry of stories that reveal the triumphs and tragedies of our ancestors. In "Empires in Love and War," I aim to bring these stories to life, to make history come alive for you in a new and exciting way.

I hope that you will enjoy this journey with me and that you will be inspired by the stories and characters you encounter. Whether you are a history buff or simply someone who loves a good tale, I think you'll find something to enjoy on these pages.

Thank you for joining me on this adventure, and I look forward to sharing this story with you.

Sincerely,

Tushar Raj

Preface

Welcome to "Empires in Love and War," a tale of love and war set against the backdrop of the rise and fall of great powers. This historical fiction novel takes you on a journey through the ages, where you will witness the emergence of mighty empires and the forces that brought them down.

The book aims to bring to life the political and social events that shaped history, as well as the personal stories of people caught in the midst of war and conflict. It is a tribute to the human spirit, showing the resilience of love in the face of adversity and the power of the human heart to triumph over war and hatred.

In this novel, you will meet a cast of characters who embody the spirit of their time. You will see the world through their eyes and experience their joys, sorrows, and triumphs. You will also learn about the major historical events that shaped the world and the motivations behind them.

Whether you are a history buff or just enjoy a good story, "Empires in Love and War" has something to offer. The book is accessible to readers of all backgrounds and is designed to be both educational and entertaining.

So, sit back, relax, and immerse yourself in the world of "Empires in Love and War." I hope you enjoy the journey!

Acknowledgements

Writing this book has been a journey of discovery, and I am grateful for the many people who have supported and inspired me along the way.

First and foremost, I would like to express my gratitude to my family, who have always encouraged me to follow my dreams and have been my rock through all the ups and downs of the writing process. Your love and support mean the world to me.

I would also like to extend my appreciation to the team at OpenAI, who provided me with the tools and resources necessary to bring this story to life. Your contributions have been invaluable, and I am grateful for your expertise and support.

I am also thankful for the countless historians and scholars who have dedicated their lives to studying and preserving the rich heritage of our world. Your work has provided me with a wealth of knowledge and inspiration, and I hope that this book will help to continue your legacy.

Finally, I would like to acknowledge my readers, who are the reason I write. Thank you for taking the time to journey with me through the rise and fall of empires, and for your support and feedback along the way.

Thank you all, from the bottom of my heart.

Prologue

Welcome, dear reader! We are thrilled to have you join us on this journey through history, love, and war. This book is a tale of the rise and fall of empires, set against the backdrop of some of the most tumultuous events in human history. From the heights of power to the depths of defeat, it is a story of ordinary people caught up in extraordinary times.

The historical period in which our story takes place is one of great change and upheaval. Empires rose and fell, borders shifted, and whole cultures were transformed. But amidst all this chaos, there were also moments of great beauty and joy. Love stories flourished and families were created, even in the most trying of circumstances.

At the heart of our tale are two individuals who come from vastly different worlds, but whose lives become intertwined as the events of history unfold around them. Through their experiences, we will see the impact of war and political upheaval on ordinary people, and the power of love to endure in even the most challenging of circumstances.

So, sit back, relax, and let us take you on a journey through history, love, and war. We promise it will be an adventure like no other.

CHAPTER ONE

Introduction

Welcome to "Empires in Love and War", a tale that brings to life the rise and fall of some of the most powerful empires in history. This novel takes you on a journey through the lives of individuals caught in the midst of war and political turmoil, as they navigate their way through the complexities of love and relationships.

Background on the Historical Period: The story takes place during a time of great change and upheaval, when empires were expanding their territories and vying for power. This was a time of war, political intrigue, and cultural exchange. It was a period when the world was rapidly evolving, and the actions of the major powers had far-reaching consequences for the future.

Overview of the Story: The novel begins with the rise of the major powers, as they seek to establish their dominance and control over new territories. As the empires grow, the individuals within them are caught up in the drama and excitement of war, while also navigating their personal lives and relationships. Through their experiences, we see the impact that war and politics have on love and relationships.

As the empires reach their peak, we witness their decline and eventual downfall, as internal conflicts and outside pressures lead to their collapse. The novel concludes with a reflection on the historical significance of these events and a consideration of the lessons learned from the rise and fall of these great powers.

So come along for the ride, and immerse yourself in the world of "Empires in Love and War". This novel promises to be a thrilling journey through the past, filled with drama, passion, and adventure. We hope you enjoy the ride!

CHAPTER TWO

Rise of Empires

The world as we know it today has been shaped by the rise and fall of many great powers throughout history. The story of the rise of these empires is a fascinating one, filled with battles, conquests, and political maneuvering. In this chapter, we'll take a closer look at the emergence of some of the major powers that dominated the world stage during the historical period we're exploring.

A. The Emergence of Major Powers

It's amazing to think about how many different empires have come and gone over the centuries. Some were small and only lasted a few years, while others lasted for centuries and shaped the world as we know it today. The empires we'll be focusing on in this story rose to prominence in the early centuries of the common era.

One of the first major powers to emerge was the Roman Empire. This vast empire stretched across much of Europe and parts of the Middle East and North Africa. The Romans were known for their incredible military power, and they used this strength to conquer many different lands and peoples.

Another major power that emerged during this time was the Chinese Empire. The Chinese were known for their advanced culture and technological innovations, and they dominated much of East Asia for centuries. They were also known for their incredible trade network, which allowed them to build wealth and influence throughout the region.

B. Expansion and Conquest

As these empires rose to power, they began to expand their territories through conquests and colonization. The Romans, for example, conquered much of Europe and parts of the Middle East and North Africa. They created a vast network of roads and infrastructure that allowed them to maintain control over these lands and to easily move troops and supplies around the empire.

The Chinese, meanwhile, were also expanding their territories through colonization and trade. They established colonies throughout East Asia and Southeast Asia, and they also built a vast network of trade routes that stretched across the region. This allowed them to build wealth and influence, and to control important trade centers and ports.

C. Political and Economic Development

As these empires grew, they also developed complex political and economic systems. The Romans, for example, had a sophisticated government that was divided into different branches, each with its own responsibilities. They also had a strong economy that was based on agriculture, trade, and manufacturing.

The Chinese, meanwhile, had a complex political system that was based on a meritocracy. They believed that people should be selected for government positions based on their abilities, rather than their social status. They also had a strong economy that was based on agriculture, trade, and manufacturing, and they were known for their advanced technological innovations.

In conclusion, the rise of empires was a critical period in world history, as these great powers emerged and dominated the world stage. They expanded their territories through conquests and colonization, and they developed sophisticated political and economic systems that allowed them to maintain control and build wealth and influence. In the next chapter, we'll take a closer look at love in the midst of war and how these great powers were affected by the complex relationships that developed during this time.

CHAPTER THREE

Love in War

In the midst of all the political maneuvering, battles, and conquests that took place during the rise of empires, there were also many stories of love and relationships. These stories humanize the events of history and remind us of the personal and emotional impact that war and conflict can have. In this chapter, we'll take a closer look at some of the love stories that developed during this historical period.

A. Meetings of the Main Characters

It's amazing to think about how two people from different worlds can come together and fall in love. That's exactly what happened in many of the love stories during the rise of empires. The main characters in these stories often met in the midst of battles or political negotiations, and despite their different backgrounds and the tensions between their countries, they found love and happiness together.

B. Relationships and Love Stories

The love stories during this historical period were often challenging, as the characters had to navigate the political tensions and conflicts between their countries. In many cases, they had to make difficult choices and sacrifices in order to be together. But despite the obstacles they faced, they persevered and found happiness and love in each other.

For example, there was a story of a Roman soldier and a Chinese princess who fell in love while the Roman Empire was at war with the Chinese Empire. Despite the political tensions between their countries, they found a way to be together and start a new life. They had to face many challenges and obstacles, but in the end, their love conquered all.

C. The Impact of War on Love

Of course, not all of the love stories during this period had happy endings. War and conflict often separated the characters, or even took their lives. The impact of war on love and relationships was devastating, and it serves as a reminder of the human toll that conflict can take.

For example, there was a story of a couple who fell in love during a battle between the Romans and the Chinese. They had to be separated when the war broke out, and they never saw each other again. The impact of war on their love was devastating, and it serves as a reminder of the human cost of conflict.

In conclusion, the love stories that developed during the rise of empires are a critical aspect of this historical period. They remind us of the personal and emotional impact that war and conflict can have, and they also show us the power of love and the lengths people will go to in order to be together. In the next chapter, we'll take a closer look at the fall of empires and the reasons behind their downfall.

CHAPTER FOUR

Fall of Empires

Just as the rise of empires was a fascinating and transformative period in world history, so too was the fall of these great powers. The fall of an empire is always a complex and multi-faceted process, and there are many different factors that can contribute to its downfall. In this chapter, we'll take a closer look at the decline and collapse of some of the major powers that we've been exploring.

A. Decline and Collapse of Powers

The fall of an empire is a slow and gradual process, and it's often the result of many different factors coming together. For the Roman Empire, for example, the decline was due in part to internal factors such as economic instability, political corruption, and military weakness. Additionally, the empire was faced with external threats from invading barbarian tribes and from declining trade with the East.

The Chinese Empire, meanwhile, faced different challenges. Despite their impressive technological innovations and strong economy, the empire was plagued by internal strife, political corruption, and a declining population. Additionally, the empire was faced with external threats from nomadic tribes and from declining trade with the West.

B. Loss of Territory and Influence

As empires decline, they also begin to lose territory and influence. The Roman Empire, for example, gradually lost control over its vast territories, and much of Europe was eventually taken over by barbarian tribes. The Chinese Empire, meanwhile, lost control over much of its colonial holdings and was eventually replaced by a series of smaller dynasties.

C. Causes of the Downfall

The causes of the fall of empires are complex and multifaceted, and they can be due to a variety of internal and external factors. Some of the most common causes include economic instability, political corruption, military weakness, declining populations, and external threats from invading tribes or declining trade with other regions.

In conclusion, the fall of empires was a critical period in world history, as these great powers declined and eventually collapsed. The loss of territory and influence had a profound impact on the world, and it paved the way for new powers to emerge and shape the future of the world. In the next chapter, we'll take a closer look at the lessons learned from the rise and fall of empires and how these lessons can be applied to our own world today.

CHAPTER FIVE

Conclusion

In this story, we've explored the rise and fall of empires and the impact of love in the midst of war. This is a fascinating period in world history, full of battles, conquests, and complex relationships. As we come to the end of our journey, let's take a moment to reflect on the historical significance of these events and the lessons we can learn from them.

A. Reflection on the Historical Significance

The rise and fall of empires is a critical chapter in world history. These great powers dominated the world stage, expanded their territories, and shaped the world as we know it today. They also provide us with an opportunity to reflect on the nature of power, the forces that drive empires to rise and fall, and the impact that these events have had on the world.

B. Lessons Learned from the Rise and Fall of Empires

The rise and fall of empires provides us with a number of important lessons. For example, we can learn about the importance of military power, the impact of political and economic systems, and the forces that drive empires to expand and conquer new lands. We can also see how these great powers were affected by love and relationships, and how these complex relationships played a role in shaping the course of history.

C. Final Thoughts on Love and War

Finally, it's important to remember that love and relationships are a powerful force in the world, even in the midst of war. As we've seen in this story, love can have a profound impact on the course of history, shaping the actions of individuals and nations, and influencing the outcome of battles and wars. As we come to the end of our journey, let's remember that love and relationships are a critical part of our world, and that they will continue to shape the course of history for generations to come.

In conclusion, the rise and fall of empires is a fascinating period in world history, and we hope that this story has provided you with a deeper understanding of the forces that drive empires to rise and fall and the impact that love and relationships can have in the midst of war. We encourage you to continue your journey of exploration and discovery, and to never stop learning about the world and its rich history.

CHAPTER SIX

Appendix

In this chapter, we'll provide some additional resources and information that will help you better understand the story of the rise and fall of empires and the impact of love in war. Whether you're a history buff or simply interested in learning more about this fascinating period, this appendix has something for everyone.

A. Glossary of Terms

In order to fully understand the story of the rise and fall of empires, it's helpful to have a basic understanding of some of the key terms and concepts. To that end, we've included a glossary of terms that will help you get up to speed on the basics. Here are a few key terms to get you started:

1. Empire: A large political unit, typically composed of many countries or territories, that is controlled by a single government.

2. Conquest: The act of gaining control over a country or territory through military force.

3. Colonization: The act of establishing a settlement in a new land and exerting control over it.

4. Meritocracy: A political system in which people are selected for government positions based on their abilities and qualifications, rather than their social status.

B. List of Key Figures and Historical Events

To help you get a better understanding of the story of the rise and fall of empires, we've included a list of key figures and historical events that you should be familiar with. Here are a few to get you started:

1. Julius Caesar: A Roman general and statesman who played a critical role in the rise of the Roman Empire.

2. Emperor Wu of Han: A Chinese emperor who ruled from 141 to 87 BCE and was known for his military conquests and for his support of the arts and sciences.

3. The Fall of the Western Roman Empire: A major event in world history that took place in 476 CE, when the Western Roman Empire collapsed and was replaced by a series of smaller kingdoms.

4. The Opium Wars: Two wars fought between China and Britain in the mid-19th century over the opium trade.

C. Further Reading and Resources

If you're interested in learning more about the rise and fall of empires and the impact of love in war, there are plenty of great resources available. Here are a few to get you started:

1. History books: There are many books available that explore the rise and fall of empires in-depth, and they are a great resource for anyone looking to learn more about this fascinating period.

2. Documentaries: There are also many documentaries available that explore the rise and fall of empires and the impact of love in war, and they are a great way to get a visual understanding of these events.

3. Websites: There are many websites that provide information on the rise and fall of empires and the impact of love in war, and they can be a great resource for anyone looking to learn more about this period in history.

In conclusion, the appendix is a great resource for anyone looking to learn more about the rise and fall of empires and the impact of love in war. Whether you're a history buff or simply interested in learning more about this fascinating period, this chapter provides a wealth of information and resources that will help you get up to speed on the basics.

Printed by Libri Plureos GmbH in Hamburg,
Germany